Scary Fairy Tales

The Little Mermaid

and other stories

Compiled by Vic Parker

Miles
Kelly

First published in 2012 by Miles Kelly Publishing Ltd
Harding's Barn, Bardfield End Green, Thaxted, Essex, CM6 3PX, UK

2 4 6 8 10 9 7 5 3 1

Publishing Director Belinda Gallagher
Creative Director Jo Cowan
Editor Sarah Parkin
Designer Jo Cowan
Editorial Assistants Lauren White, Amy Johnson
Production Manager Elizabeth Collins
Reprographics Stephan Davis, Jennifer Hunt, Thom Allaway

ISBN 978-1-84810-586-7

Printed in China

British Library Cataloguing-in-Publication Data
A catalogue record for this book is available from the British Library

ACKNOWLEDGEMENTS

The publishers would like to thank the following artists who have contributed to this book:

Cover: Iva Sasheva at The Bright Agency
Advocate Art: Luke Finlayson
The Bright Agency: Peter Cottrill, Gerald Kelley
Duncan Smith

All other artwork from the Miles Kelly Artwork Bank

The publishers would like to thank the following source for the use of their photographs:
Shutterstock.com (cover) donatas1205, Eky Studio; (page decorations) alarik,
Ensuper, Eugene Ivanov, lejlek

Every effort has been made to acknowledge the source and copyright holder of each picture.
Miles Kelly Publishing apologises for any unintentional errors or omissions.

Made with paper from a sustainable forest

www.mileskelly.net   info@mileskelly.net

www.factsforprojects.com

Contents

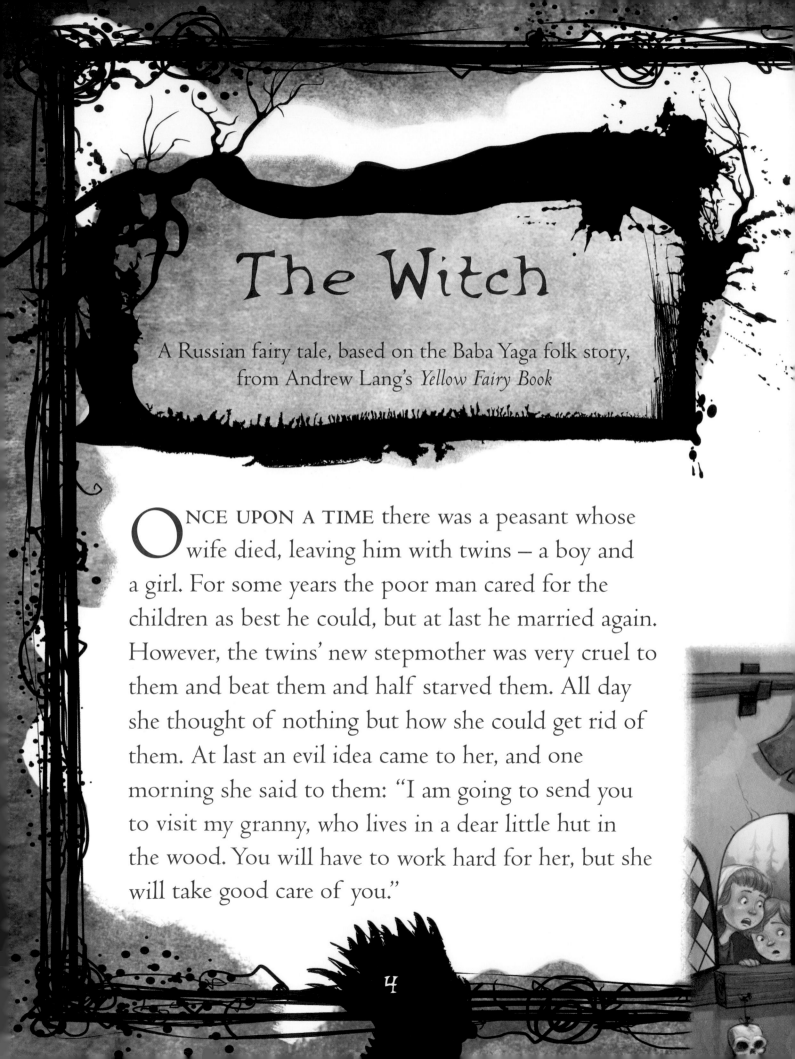

The Witch

A Russian fairy tale, based on the Baba Yaga folk story,
from Andrew Lang's *Yellow Fairy Book*

ONCE UPON A TIME there was a peasant whose
wife died, leaving him with twins – a boy and
a girl. For some years the poor man cared for the
children as best he could, but at last he married again.
However, the twins' new stepmother was very cruel to
them and beat them and half starved them. All day
she thought of nothing but how she could get rid of
them. At last an evil idea came to her, and one
morning she said to them: "I am going to send you
to visit my granny, who lives in a dear little hut in
the wood. You will have to work hard for her, but she
will take good care of you."

So the children left the house, with only a bottle of milk and a piece of ham and a hunk of bread. The little sister, who was very wise for her years, said to the brother, "Our stepmother is not sending us to her granny, but to a wicked witch. We must be polite and kind to everyone, and never touch a crumb belonging to anyone else. Then, who knows, someone might help us." And they struck out into the great gloomy wood.

Eventually, the children saw in the thickest of the trees a little hut. Nervously they peeped inside – and there lay the witch, with her head on the threshold, a foot in each corner and her knees cocked up, almost touching the ceiling. "Who's there?" she snarled.

Though the twins were terrified, they answered politely. "Good morning, Granny. Our stepmother has sent us to serve you."

"See that you do it well, then," growled the witch. "If I am pleased with you, I'll reward you, but if I am not, I'll cook you in the oven!"

So saying, she set the girl down to spin yarn, and she gave the boy a sieve in which to carry water from the well, and she herself went out into the wood.

The girl began weeping bitterly because she could not spin. But suddenly she heard hundreds of little feet, and from every hole in the hut mice came pattering, squeaking and saying:

"Little girl, why are your eyes so red?

If you want help, then give us some bread."

And the girl gave them some of her bread. Then the mice told her that the witch had a cat, and the cat was very fond of ham. If she would give the cat her ham, it would show her the way out of the wood, and in the meantime they would spin the yarn for her. So the girl set out to look for the cat, and, as she was

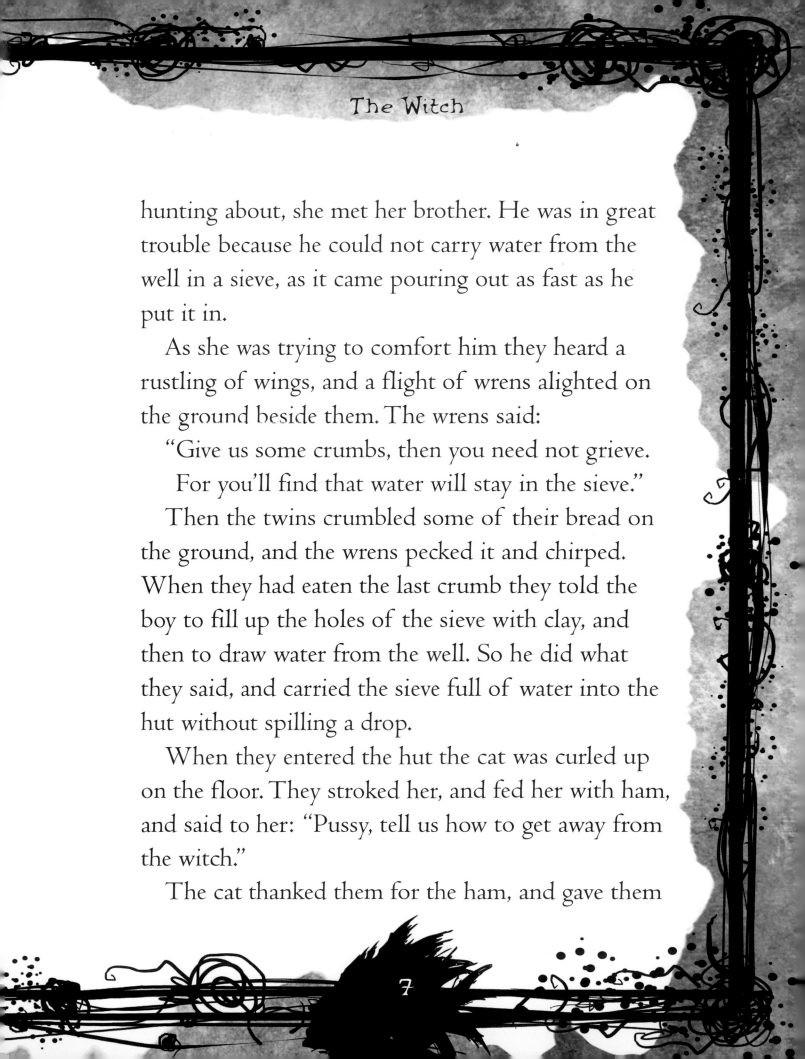

hunting about, she met her brother. He was in great trouble because he could not carry water from the well in a sieve, as it came pouring out as fast as he put it in.

As she was trying to comfort him they heard a rustling of wings, and a flight of wrens alighted on the ground beside them. The wrens said:

"Give us some crumbs, then you need not grieve.

For you'll find that water will stay in the sieve."

Then the twins crumbled some of their bread on the ground, and the wrens pecked it and chirped. When they had eaten the last crumb they told the boy to fill up the holes of the sieve with clay, and then to draw water from the well. So he did what they said, and carried the sieve full of water into the hut without spilling a drop.

When they entered the hut the cat was curled up on the floor. They stroked her, and fed her with ham, and said to her: "Pussy, tell us how to get away from the witch."

The cat thanked them for the ham, and gave them

a pocket-handkerchief and a comb, and told the children what they should do with them to escape. The cat had scarcely finished speaking when the witch returned.

"Well, you have done well enough for today," she grumbled, "but tomorrow you'll have something more difficult to do, and if you don't do it well, straight into the oven you go."

Half dead with fright, the poor children lay down to sleep on a heap of straw in the corner of the hut. They dared not close their eyes and scarcely breathed.

In the morning the witch gave the girl two pieces of linen to weave before night, and the boy a pile of wood to chop. Then the witch left them to their tasks and went out into the wood.

As soon as she was out of sight the children took the comb and the handkerchief and, holding hands, they ran, and ran, and ran. First they met the witch's watchdog, who was going to tear them to pieces, but they threw the remains of their bread to him, and he ate it and wagged his tail. Then they were hindered by the birch trees, whose branches almost put their eyes out. But the little sister tied the twigs together with her hair ribbon, and they got past safely and came out on to the open fields.

In the meantime, in the hut, the cat was busy weaving the linen. The witch returned to see how the children were getting on, and she crept up to the window and whispered: "Are you weaving, my dear?"

"Yes, Granny, I am weaving," answered the cat.

Then the witch realised that the children had escaped! She was furious and hit the cat, screeching: "Why did you let the children leave the hut?"

But the cat spat and answered: "I have served you all these years and you never even threw me a bone, but the children gave me their own piece of ham."

Then the witch was furious with the watchdog and with the birch trees, because they had let the children pass. But the dog answered: "I have served you all these years and you never gave me so much as a crust, but the children gave me their own loaf of bread."

And the birch rustled its leaves and said: "I have

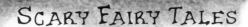

served you longer than I can say, and you never even tied a bit of twine round my branches, but the children bound them up with their bright ribbon."

So the witch saw there was no help to be got from her old servants, and she mounted her broom and set off after the children herself. As the twins ran they heard the sound of the broom close behind them. They remembered what the cat had told them and threw the handkerchief over their shoulders. Instantly, a deep, broad river flowed behind them.

It took the witch a long time to find a place to ride over on her broomstick, but at last she got across, and continued the chase faster than before.

As the children ran they heard the broom close behind them, so, quick as thought, they did what the cat had told them and threw the comb down on the ground. In an instant, a dense forest sprang up, in which the roots and branches were so closely intertwined, that it was impossible to force a way through it. When the witch came to it she found that there was nothing for it but to turn round and go

back to her hut, tearing her hair with rage.

The twins ran straight on till they reached home. They told their father all that they had suffered, and he was so angry with their stepmother that he drove her out of the house and never let her return. Then he and the children lived happily ever after.

Aladdin and the Wonderful Lamp

An extract from *The Arabian Nights Entertainments*,
retold by Andrew Lang

THERE ONCE LIVED a poor tailor, who had a son called Aladdin, a careless, idle boy who would do nothing but play all day long in the streets with little idle boys like himself. This so grieved the father that he died; yet, in spite of his mother's tears and prayers, Aladdin did not mend his ways. One day, when he was playing in the streets as usual, a stranger asked him his age and if he was the son of Mustapha the tailor.

"I am, sir," replied Aladdin; "but he died a long while ago."

On this the stranger, who was a famous African

magician, hugged him and kissed him, saying: "I am your uncle! I recognised you because you look so like my brother. You must go to your mother and tell her I am coming."

Aladdin ran home, and told his mother of his newly found uncle.

"Indeed, child," she said, "your father had a brother, but I always thought he was dead."

However, she prepared supper, and told Aladdin to get ready to welcome his uncle. The strange man came laden with gifts of wine and fruit. He kissed the place where Mustapha used to sit, bidding Aladdin's mother not to be surprised at not having seen him before, as he had been out of the country for forty years. He then turned to Aladdin and asked him his trade, at which the boy hung his head, while his mother burst into tears. On learning that Aladdin was idle and refused to learn a trade, he offered to rent a shop for him and stock it for him. The very next day he bought Aladdin a fine suit of clothes, and took him all over the city, showing him the sights. At

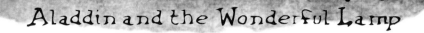

nightfall, he brought Aladdin home to his mother, who was overjoyed to see her son so fine.

On the following day, he led Aladdin into some beautiful gardens a long way outside the city gates. They sat down by a fountain, and the magician pulled a cake from his girdle, which he divided between them. They then journeyed onwards till they almost reached the mountains. Aladdin was so tired that he begged to go back, but the magician won him over with pleasant stories, and led him on.

At last they came to two mountains divided by a narrow valley.

"We will go no farther," said the false uncle. "I will show you something wonderful; you gather up sticks while I kindle a fire."

When it was lit the magician threw a powder on it, at the same time saying some magical words. The earth trembled a little and opened in front of them to show a square, flat stone with a brass ring in the middle to raise it by. Aladdin tried to run away, but the magician caught him and gave him a blow that knocked him down.

"What have I done, uncle?" Aladdin begged.

The magician replied, more kindly: "Fear nothing, but obey me. Beneath this stone lies a treasure which is to be yours, and no one else may touch it, so you must do exactly as I tell you."

At the word 'treasure', Aladdin forgot his fears, and grasped the ring as he was told, saying the names of his father and grandfather. The stone came up quite easily and some steps appeared.

"Go down," said the magician; "at the foot of those steps you will find an open door leading into three large halls. Tuck up your gown and go through them without touching anything, or you will die instantly. These halls lead into a garden of fine fruit trees. Walk on till you come to an alcove in a terrace where stands a lighted lamp. Pour out the oil it contains and bring the lamp to me."

The magician drew a ring from his finger and gave it to Aladdin, wishing him good luck.

Nervously, Aladdin crept down the stairs. He found everything just as the magician had said. He gathered some fruit off the trees, got the lamp, and hurried back to the mouth of the cave.

The magician cried out: "Make haste and give me the lamp."

But Aladdin was suspicious. "Only when I'm safely out of the cave," he yelled back.

The magician flew into a terrible rage. Throwing some more powder on the fire, he said more magic words, and the stone rolled back into its place.

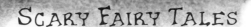

The magician left Persia for ever, which plainly showed that he was no uncle of Aladdin's. He was a cunning magician who had read in his magic books of a wonderful lamp, which would make him the most powerful man in the world. Though he alone knew where to find it, he could only receive it from the hand of another. He had picked out the foolish Aladdin for this purpose, intending to get the lamp and kill him afterwards.

For two days Aladdin remained in the dark, crying and wailing. At last he clasped his hands in prayer, and in doing so rubbed the ring, which the magician had forgotten to take from him. Immediately an enormous and frightful genie rose out of it, saying: "What do you want from me? I am the Slave of the Ring, and will obey you in all things."

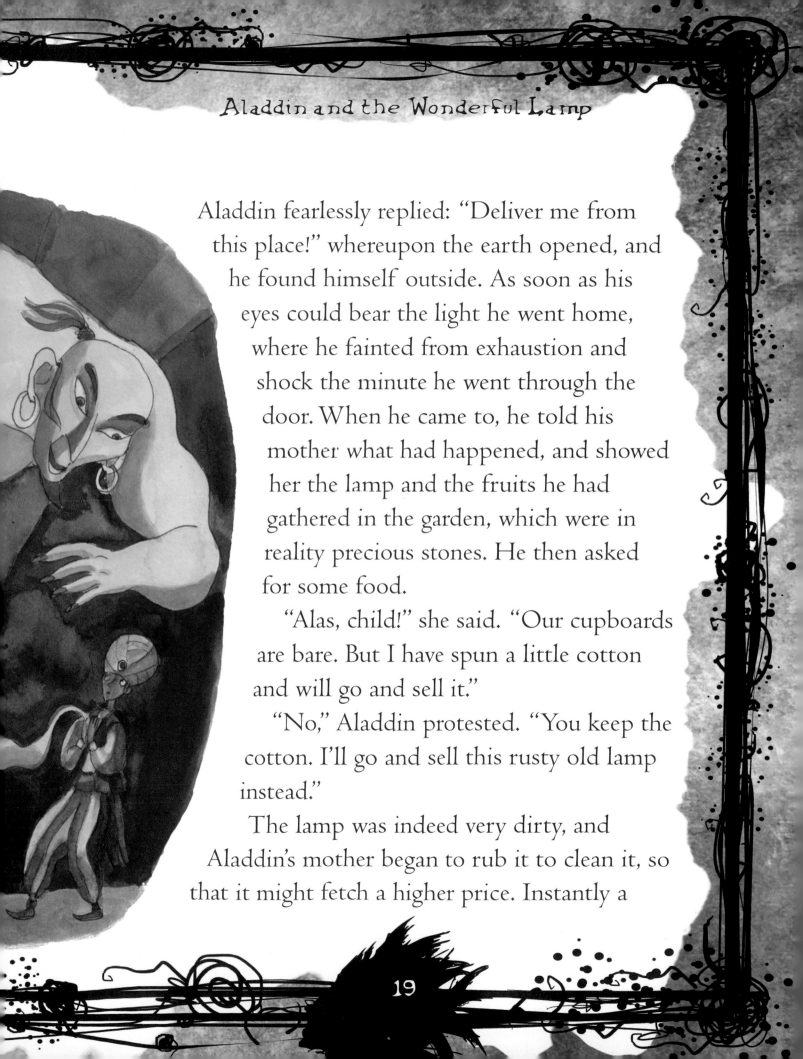

Aladdin fearlessly replied: "Deliver me from this place!" whereupon the earth opened, and he found himself outside. As soon as his eyes could bear the light he went home, where he fainted from exhaustion and shock the minute he went through the door. When he came to, he told his mother what had happened, and showed her the lamp and the fruits he had gathered in the garden, which were in reality precious stones. He then asked for some food.

"Alas, child!" she said. "Our cupboards are bare. But I have spun a little cotton and will go and sell it."

"No," Aladdin protested. "You keep the cotton. I'll go and sell this rusty old lamp instead."

The lamp was indeed very dirty, and Aladdin's mother began to rub it to clean it, so that it might fetch a higher price. Instantly a

hideous genie appeared, and asked what she wanted. She fainted, but Aladdin, snatching the lamp, said boldly: "Fetch us something to eat!"

The genie returned with a silver bowl, twelve silver plates containing rich meats, two silver cups, and two bottles of wine.

Aladdin's mother came to and couldn't believe her eyes. "Wherever did all this come from?" she said.

"Don't ask, just eat," Aladdin replied, grinning.

So they sat and tucked in, and Aladdin told his mother about the lamp. She begged him to sell it, and have nothing to do with devils.

"No," said Aladdin, "luck has brought it to me, so we will use it – and the ring too."

When they had eaten everything the genie had brought, Aladdin sold the silver plates. He then summoned the genie, who gave him another set of plates – and thus they lived for many years.

How Bradamante Conquered the Wizard

From Andrew Lang's *Red Romance Book*

FROM CHILDHOOD, Bradamante had loved play-fighting with swords and bows and arrows, and her main joy was to mount the most fiery horses in her father's stable. So as well as growing up beautiful, she became tall and strong. She liked to put on men's armour and take part in tournaments among the most valiant knights. In fact, it was rare that she failed to carry off the prize.

Of course so wise and beautiful a maiden had no lack of wooers, but Bradamante wasn't interested in any of them — except the brave Sir Roger. But she kept her love secret and was content to wait till Roger

thought fit to claim her as his bride.

One day, Bradamante heard the news that Roger had disappeared, and no one knew where. She didn't weep nor wail nor even utter a word, but the next morning she sharpened her sword and fastened her helmet and rode off to seek him.

Through many adventures, she pushed on till she crossed a mountain, and reached a valley watered by a stream and shaded by trees. There on the bank lay a young man with his head buried in his hands and seemingly in deepest misery. He told Bradamante that he had been out riding with a damsel whom he had lately freed from the power of a dragon. He had hoped to marry the lady, but as they rode along, a winged horse guided by a man in black swooped down and snatched her away.

"Since that day," he explained, "I have sought her through forests and over mountains, wherever I heard that a wizard's den was to be found. But each time it was a false hope that lured me on. Now, I am sure that my beloved is held captive among the rocky slopes nearby — but I am at a loss how to rescue her."

"If it is there she lies, I will free her," cried Bradamante; but the knight shook his head.

"I have visited that dark and dreadful place," he said. "It is like the valley of death. Among black and pathless precipices stands a rock, and on its top is a castle whose walls are of steel. It was built, so I have since learned, by a magician, and none can capture it. I have watched two knights try and fail — one was Gradasso, King of Sericane, and the other (and the more valiant) was the noble young Sir Roger."

Bradamante's heart leaped at the mention of Roger, but she only said, "What happened to them?"

"I told them my sad tale, and they answered in knightly fashion that they would fight for the freedom of my lady. The king tried to attack the castle first, but in an instant there shot into the sky the winged horse bearing his master, clad as before in black armour. He darted down, and thrust a spear into Gradasso's side. Roger ran to help, never thinking of what might befall himself. But, in truth, how could mortal men fight with a wizard who had studied all the magic of the East, and had a winged horse to help him? His movements were so swift that they couldn't see where to strike him, and soon both Gradasso and Roger were covered with wounds, while their enemy had never once been touched.

"Their strength as well as their courage began to fail against this strange warfare. Then the wizard drew a silken covering from off his shield and held the shield towards them as a mirror. It blazed so bright that I had to cover my eyes, and when I opened them again, I was alone upon the mountain. Roger and Gradasso had doubtless been carried by the wizard to the dark cells of the prison, where my fair lady also lies," answered the knight, and he again dropped his head upon his hands.

Now this knight was a wicked man called Count Pinabello, but Bradamante did not know that she shouldn't trust him.

"Please, take me to the castle," she cried, thinking joyfully that her quest to find Roger was at an end.

"I will lead you there, if
you so desire to meet certain doom,"
answered the knight, with an evil glint in his eye.

So they set forth, but Pinabello did not lead
Bradamante to the castle. Instead, he led her to the
mouth of a dark, steep cavern – and then he pushed
her down!

Bradamante tumbled to the very bottom and lay there for a while, bruised and shaken. When she became used to the darkness, she stood up and looked around. 'There may be some way out,' she thought, noting that the cave was less gloomy than she had fancied, and felt round the walls. On one side there seemed to be a passage, and going cautiously down it she found that it ended in a sort of church, with a lamp hanging over the altar.

At this moment there opened a little gate, and through it came a lady. She was bare-footed, with streaming hair.

"Oh Bradamante," she said, "I have waited a long time for you. Here lies the tomb of the great magician Merlin. Before he died, he said that one day you would find your way here. He commanded me to come here from a far-distant land and help you."

At that, a voice rose up from the tomb nearby, where Merlin had laid buried for many hundreds of years. "It is foretold that you will be the wife of Roger," it boomed. "So take courage and follow the path that leads you to him. Let nothing turn you aside until you have overthrown the wizard who holds him captive."

Then the voice ceased, and the lady explained that she was Melissa, a kind sorceress who went through the world seeking to set wrongs right. She showed Bradamante a book that foretold all the glories that her's and Roger's children would achieve.

"Tomorrow at dawn," she said when she had finished and put away the magic scroll, "I myself will lead you to the wizard's castle."

Next morning Melissa and Bradamante rode out from the cavern. They passed over rushing rivers, and climbed high precipices, and as they went Melissa taught Bradamante how to try to set Roger free.

"No man, however brave, could withstand the wizard, who has his magic mirror as well as his flying horse to aid him. If you would reach Roger, you must first get possession of a ring owned by a man called Brunello, who is riding only a few miles in front of us. In the presence of this ring all charms and sorceries lose their power; but, take heed, for to outwit Brunello is no easy task."

"It is good fortune indeed that Brunello should be so near us," answered Bradamante joyfully; "but how shall I obtain his ring?"

"You must fall to talking with him upon magic and enchantments," replied Melissa, "but beware lest he guess who you are or what you want. Lead him on till he offers to guide you to the wizard's castle. As you go, strike him dead, before he can spy into your heart, and, above all, before he can slip the ring into his mouth. If he does that, you will lose Roger for ever."

Having said all this Melissa bade Bradamante farewell, and they parted with tears and promises of meeting again speedily. Bradamante entered an inn close by, where Brunello was already seated. She knew who he was straight away — but he knew her too, for many a time he had seen her at jousts and tournaments. Both pretending not to know each other, they fell into talk, and discussed the castle and the knights who lay imprisoned inside.

"I have dared to try many perilous adventures," said Bradamante at length, "and I have never failed to trample my foes underfoot. If only I had a guide to take me to the castle, I myself would challenge this wizard to deadly combat."

Brunello offered his own services and together they climbed the mountain till they stood at the foot of the castle. "Look at those walls of steel that crown the precipice," began Brunello; but before he could say more a strong girdle was passed round his arms, which were fastened tightly to his sides. In spite of his cries and struggles, Bradamante drew the ring off his finger and placed it on her own, though kill him she would not. Then she seized a horn which hung nearby from a cord and, blowing a loud blast, waited calmly for the magician to answer.

Out he came on his flying steed, bearing on his left arm his silken-covered shield, while he uttered spells that had laid low many a knight and lady. Bradamante heard them all, and was not any the worse for the most evil of them.

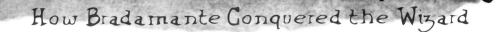

Furious at his defeat, the wizard snatched the cover
from the shield, and Bradamante, knowing full well
what was to follow, sank heavily on the ground. At
this the wizard covered his shield once more, and
guided his steed swiftly to where the maiden lay.
After that, unclasping a chain from his body, he bent
down to find her. It was then that she lifted her
ringed hand, and saw that before her stood an old
man with white hair and a face scarred with sorrow.

"Kill me, I pray you, gentle lady," cried the
magician, "yet know before I die that it is only
because I love Roger that I have caused so much
misery to so many gallant knights and fair damsels.
I am Atlantes, the servant whose job it was to watch
over him in childhood and use my magical powers to
keep him from harm. As Roger grew to manhood, he
was always the bravest and best in deeds of chivalry.
So reckless was he, that many a time it needed all my
magic to bring him back to life when seemingly he lay
dead. At length, to keep him from harm, I built this
castle, and filled it with all that was beautiful, and

with knights and ladies to be his companions. When everything was ready I captured Roger himself. Now, take my horse and shield, and throw open wide the castle doors – do what you will, but leave me Roger."

The heart of Bradamante was not usually deaf to the sorrows of others, but this time it seemed turned to stone.

"I have won your horse and shield," she said. "You should have learned that it is useless to war against fate. Fate has given you into my hands. Therefore, lead the way to the gate, and I will follow you."

They climbed in silence the long flight of steps leading to the castle; then Atlantes stooped and raised a stone on which was engraved strange and magic signs. Beneath the stone was a row of pots filled with undying flames, and on these the wizard let the stone fall. In a moment there was a sound as if all the rocks on the earth were split, the castle vanished into the air, and with it Atlantes.

Instead, a troop of knights and ladies stood before Bradamante, who saw and heard only Roger.

The Little Mermaid

An extract from the tale by Hans Christian Andersen

THE LITTLE MERMAID went out from her garden, and took the road to the foaming whirlpools, behind which the sorceress lived. She had never been that way before: neither flowers nor grass grew there; nothing but bare, grey, sandy ground stretched out to the whirlpools, where the water, like foaming mill-wheels, whirled round everything that it seized, and cast it into the fathomless deep. Through the midst of these crushing whirlpools the little mermaid was obliged to pass, to reach the dominions of the sea witch; and also for a long distance the only road lay right across a quantity of warm, bubbling

mire, called by the witch her turfmoor. Beyond this stood her house, in the centre of a strange forest, in which all the trees and flowers were polypi – half animals and half plants; they looked like serpents with a hundred heads growing out of the ground. The branches were long slimy arms, with fingers like flexible worms, moving limb after limb from the root to the top. All that could be reached in the sea they seized, and held fast, so that it never escaped from their clutches.

The little mermaid was so alarmed at what she saw, that her heart beat with fear, and she was very nearly turning back; but she thought of the

prince, and of the human soul for which she longed, and her courage returned. She fastened her long, flowing hair round her head, so that the polypi might not seize hold of it. Then she darted forward as a fish shoots through the water, between the supple arms and fingers of the ugly polypi, which were stretched out on each side of her. She saw that each held in its grasp something it had seized with its numerous little arms. The white skeletons of human beings who had perished at sea, and had sunk down into the deep waters, skeletons of land animals, oars, rudders, and chests of ships were lying tightly grasped by their clinging arms; even a mermaid, whom they had caught and strangled, and this seemed the most shocking of all to the little princess.

She now came to a space of marshy ground in the wood, where large, fat water-snakes were rolling in the mire, and showing their ugly, drab-coloured bodies. In the midst of this spot stood a house, built with the bones of shipwrecked human beings. There sat the sea witch, allowing a toad to eat from her mouth. She called the ugly water-snakes her little chickens, and allowed them to crawl all over her.

"I know what you want," said the sea witch. "It is very stupid of you, but you shall have your way. You want to get rid of your fish's tail, and to have two supports instead of it, like human beings on earth, so that the young prince may fall in love with you, and that you may have an immortal soul." And then the witch laughed so loud and disgustingly, that the toad and the snakes fell to the ground, and lay there wriggling about. "You are just in time," said the witch; "for after sunrise tomorrow I should not be able to help you till the end of another year. I will prepare a magic potion for you, with which you must swim to land tomorrow before sunrise, and sit down on the shore and drink it. Your tail will disappear, and shrink up into what mankind calls legs, and you will feel great pain, as if a sword were passing through you. But all who see you will say that you are the prettiest little human being they ever saw. You will have the same floating gracefulness of movement, and no dancer will ever tread so lightly; but at every step you take it will feel as if you were treading upon sharp knives, and that the blood must flow. If you will bear all this, I will help you."

"Yes, I will," said the princess in a trembling voice, as she thought of the prince and the immortal soul.

"But think again," said the witch; "for once your shape has become like a human being, you can no more be a mermaid. You will never return through the water to your sisters, or to your father's palace again; and if you do not win the love of the prince, so that he is willing to forget his father and mother for your sake, and to love you with his whole soul, and allow

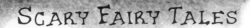

the priest to join your hands that you may be man and wife, then you will never have an immortal soul. The first morning after he marries another your heart will break, and you will become foam on the crest of the waves."

"I will do it," said the little mermaid, and she became pale as death.

"But I must be paid also," said the witch, "and it is not a trifle that I ask. You have the sweetest voice of any who dwell here in the depths of the sea, and you believe that you will be able to charm the prince with it also, but this voice you must give to me; the best thing you possess will I have for the price of my draught. My own blood must be mixed with it, that it may be as sharp as a two-edged sword."

"But if you take away my voice," said the little mermaid, "what is left for me?"

"Your beautiful form, your graceful walk, and your expressive eyes; surely with these you can enchain a man's heart. Well, have you lost your courage? Put out your little

tongue that I may cut it off as my payment; and then you shall have the powerful draught."

"It shall be," said the little mermaid.

Then the witch placed her cauldron on the fire to prepare the magic potion.

"Cleanliness is a good thing," said she, scouring the vessel with snakes, which she had tied together in a large knot; then she pricked herself in the breast, and let the black blood drop into it. The steam that rose formed itself into such horrible shapes that no one could look at them without fear. Every moment the witch threw something else into the vessel, and when it at last began to boil, the sound was like the weeping of a crocodile. When at last the magic potion was ready, it looked like the clearest water. "There it is for you," said the witch. Then she cut off the mermaid's tongue, so that she became dumb, and would never again speak or sing.

"If the polypi should seize hold of you as you return through the wood," said the witch, "throw over them a few drops of the potion, and their fingers will be torn into a thousand pieces." But the little mermaid had no occasion to do this, for the polypi sprang back in terror when they caught sight of the glittering potion, which shone in her hand like a twinkling star.

So she passed quickly through the wood and the marsh, and between the rushing whirlpools. She saw that in her father's palace the torches in the ballroom were extinguished, and all within asleep; but she did not venture to go in to them, for now she was dumb and going to leave them for ever, she felt as if her heart would break. She stole into the garden, took a flower from the flowerbeds of each of her sisters, kissed her hand a thousand times towards the palace, and then rose up through the dark blue waters.